Cyril the Spider

by

Glenn J. Cranmer

Illustrated by Simon Groves

ISBN: 978-0-244-81023-8

PublishNation
www.publishnation.co.uk

For Crecella and Hannah

Cyril the Spider

Cyril was a small brown spider with stubby legs.

He could spin his silk like no other spider

and make really wonderful things.

But the other spiders weren't interested in that.

All they were interested in was ...

... who had the most flies

and who had the longest legs.

"Look, we can use this, can't we?"
Cyril said, as he walked out in the rain
with a beautiful silk umbrella.

"What's the use of that?" asked all the
other spiders. "All that matters is...

...who has the most flies

and who has the longest legs."

The next morning Cyril woke to find
his umbrella had disappeared. So, he spent
the rest of the day making more things.

"Look, we can use these, can't we?" he asked.
He had made little silk footballs and goalposts, too.

"What's the use in those?" asked the other spiders.

"All that matters is ... who has the most flies
and who has the longest legs!"

The next morning, Cyril woke to find
that his footballs and goalposts had gone too!
Just like the silk umbrella. So once again he spent
the day making more things.

"We can use this, can't we?" he said as he lay down
on a beautiful silk bed, with soft sheets and pillows.
But there was no reply. All the spiders
were too busy arguing over...

...who had the most flies

and who had the longest legs.

The next morning Cyril woke to find
all his things had gone ... again!

"Oh, it's no use!" said Cyril as he slowly
lifted his head.

"The things I make are no use to anybody.
That's why the other spiders
get rid of them."

"Just like me, they are not wanted,"
he groaned.

13

He turned his sad little face up to the sky,
and saw the honeybees, happily flying over his head.

Everyone working together.
Everyone bringing the nectar back to help each other.

"That's where I need to be?" Cyril thought.
So, he spun some silk wings and climbed to
the top of the tallest tree.

Then, with a very brave leap, he was flying!
His little legs wiggled as the breeze took him
down to the beehive.

Unfortunately for Cyril, he landed
in thick sticky honey, which the bees thought
he was trying to steal.

"STING HIM!" the worker bees shouted.

Cyril was so scared, he spun up
a silk shield in the blink of an eye
to protect himself.

"Wait!" commanded one of the bees.

Cyril looked up to see that it was the Queen Bee.

She was hovering above Cyril's luxurious

silk bed, holding Cyril's umbrella.

Behind her, worker bees were kicking Cyril's

footballs around with the baby bees.

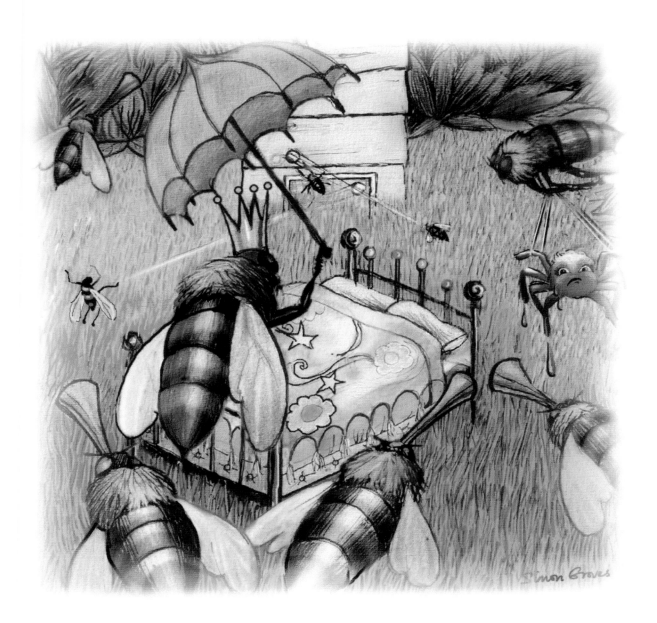

"Fairies did not make these magical things?" said the Queen. "You made them!"
A very shaky Cyril replied, "Y-yes, Your M-majesty. I made them."

The royal trumpets sounded and from all directions came ladybirds, caterpillars, bumblebees, and butterflies.

"What wonders!" they shouted. "What treasures!" they cried. "And from a spider, too?"

"Cyril, from this moment forth you shall be SIR Cyril!" proclaimed the Queen. "And I hope you will stay here, where you truly belong."

So, Cyril did stay, and he went on to
become the most famous spider ever, building
boats for bumblebees and castles
for caterpillars.

It didn't matter who had
the most flies or who had the longest legs.

He didn't have to FIT IN. He could be DIFFERENT.

With that, Cyril the spider knew...

he had found his HOME.

23

35511861R00020